C000000998

Q

CANDIA McWILLIAM

Change of Use

A
BLOOMSBURY
QUID

First published in Great Britain 1996

Copyright © 1996 by Candia McWilliam

The moral right of the author has been asserted

Bloomsbury Publishing Plc,
2 Soho Square, London W1V 6HB

A CIP catalogue record for this book
is available from the British Library

ISBN 0 7475 2896 9

Typeset by Hewer Text Composition Services,
Edinburgh
Printed by St Edmundsbury Press, Suffolk
Jacket design by Jeff Fisher

In the pantry at the back of the long house, Mary shifted back a little on the edge of the stone sink, as she had done since these Thursday rituals began. She wanted to balance so she could drift off into her own thoughts without falling in or letting Mr Charteris know that she was not fully with him as he pushed away at her with his hands wringing one another on the rattling taps behind her back. She had given him green beans for lunch for a change, instead of peas with the Thursday shepherd's pie. She could smell the blackberry and apple she was making for his dinner cooking away under its crumble in the low oven.

'Tell me your name again, my dear,' said Mr Charteris.

'Dorothy,' said Mary, to liven things up.

Overwhelmed by this unanticipated new companion, Mr Charteris shook sadly as though to rid himself of dust, buttoned, sighed, pushed Mary aside like a curtain and washed his hands under taps that quivered as the water promised to arrive, held off and then gushed out, hot and chalky, through the aged piping into the sink where tonight's potatoes eyed him smugly from the colander.

He dried his hands while Mary set the kettle to boil. Upstairs the house slept, as it would for another twenty-five minutes.

He felt astonishingly well, astonishingly.

He smelt the tea as she spooned it from the red-and-gold caddy, saw her skin it seemed to him glow with the new life Thursdays must bring her, felt the sunshine as it came in slabs through the barred deep windows of the back of the house that looked on to lawn and shrubs and finally thicket, copse and wood. No one knew the house as he did. He had been a boy here and would die here. Each room held its story for him.

Mr Charteris sat down and rested his forearms on the kitchen table.

Mary brought him a tray of old silver, some cloths and the tin of polish.

'The lid's hard,' said Mr Charteris. 'Got stuck. When it dries this stuff's like glue.'

'I'm sure you can do it,' said Mary, pouring water on to the tea leaves from the heavy kettle off the stove. She kicked herself for not having tested the lid of the polish tin. This part was as important for him as what had gone before. She was sure that these Thursdays didn't take life from him but put it back.

Maybe the care she was offering him was not orthodox, but it was natural.

'There. Done it. Nothing like experience,' said Mr Charteris.

She hoped he wouldn't look too closely at the silver on the tray. Not much of it matched and not all of it was silver. She'd brought some deliberately for him from other places she worked at.

'This tea's just the thing,' said Mr Charteris. 'Polishing dries out the tubes.'

She looked over at him from the lower oven where she was testing the crumble with a spoon. Her overall was getting tight. She shut the heavy door and bathed in the heat of butter and sugar burning together. It all made her hungry, she couldn't help it. She was hungry all the time now.

'Yes, and that is thirsty work too,' said Mr Charteris, supposing he should now pat Mary's bottom to go with the words, but not bothering to get up and go over to her actually to do this, because now came the reliable pleasure of his afternoon, the creaming and dipping and rubbing and the revelation of the silver. The distinction between his younger days and these later years was this for him: then he had been blind to the beauty of habit; now it was a luxury, a conscious indulgence as irresistible as yawning, stretching, surrendering to sleep.

Habit had become his bride, his chosen ravishment, his companion elect. It was simply that his wish to share his habit with just one other person at a time was not encouraged by the new masters here.

Mary was wondering how to keep the room empty for long enough to let Mr Charteris be through with his polishing. She relied upon the herd instinct, the set of rules that kept the rest of the residents of the house hung about their routine like a beard of bees.

He was holding up each knife to the light, checking each fork for speckles of erosion, the bruise of tarnish. To the left of the tray on the silver cloth he set the cleaned utensils, to the right lay the unpolished. The whole collection shone about as much as a dish of sardines and vinegar on toast. Still it made him so glad that she guessed he saw a shine not visible to her.

She heard the stomp and waltz of the polishing machine start up on the ballroom floor above. Along the kitchen ceiling ran wiring and pipes that made abrupt changes of direction. From hooks along the wall hung clutches of keys. A plastic fire extinguisher in a glass case sat above its predecessor, a heavy metal torpedo that said on its side 'Last Date of Service: June 1956'.

She heard a rustle in the pantry.

In there, the baleful wedges of wholesale cheese lay plastic-sealed and piled on the slate shelf. Mary reached in her hand behind one and pulled out the humane mousetrap. The creature inside flustered between its perspex chambers.

How humane was it to take the humane mousetrap to the outhouse where the cats had their hideout? She carried the fretful snack and tipped it out in front of the cat she considered to be the idlest. That way, it was fairer.

Two slow frivolous bats of its paw later, the cat was happily prolonging this small local torment.

From the back door, the kitchen

looked as it could have almost any Thursday afternoon of the century as Mr Charteris had by now often described it to her.

Mr Charteris polished away, his apron black, his extensible cuff-restrainers glistening, the cup of tea neglected. His hair was white as salt, his face of a kind that is no longer trained into being – unremarkable features withheld by years of emu-lative mimicry into an expression of checked emotion and impersonal superiority. But his eyes were a disturbingly self-willed brown, where one might have expected self-effacing blue.

Looking out from the other kitchen door facing the gates at the

front of the house and up the outer
stairway to the terrace, Mary saw
today's afternoon beginning. Two
of the older ladies were wheeled
out, a sunshade set above them, a
tea tray brought. No bell had woken
the after-lunch sleepers, but the
windows began to show move-
ment behind themselves; a few
blinds were raised. In the main
rooms, between the grave, flat-
tened, central columns of the pedi-
ment, there was the sound of dance
music, a raised voice, an insistent
hard tapping.

Among the trees on the lawn,
figures dressed just like Mary
moved between chairs and
benches, recliners covered with

rugs where still bodies lay, stirring them, sometimes with a word, sometimes a touch. They seemed to be competing with one another to awaken a sleeper. Over some of the bodies, the overalled men and women shrugged vehemently, like cricketers loosening up. It was as though there were two teams, one ghoulishly dedicated to fun and activity, the other to repose. In the wide green of the afternoon, somnolence had the worst of it for the time being but could well show form later. The classical enclosure of the park suggested an eventual triumph of sleep.

The gates in front of the house's wide face implied a fixed modesty that must prevail in the end. The house would shut itself away, a fading beauty needing sleep in order to reawaken refreshed.

Driving the laundry van in at the gates, Francis Mullard changed down at the turning off the main road, felt the cattle grid under the wheels, slowed again on turning into the asphalted back drive, and wondered if the grid kept the old folks in, too. In the back of the van the sheets were cold and heavy inside the hampers. The van had been parked in the underground car-park of the laundry, where it never got warm, even in a summer like this one.

Francis's own grandmother was living at home with them at present. Her very active ways had knocked them for six at first, but now they were used to her walking miles in the night over their heads and bringing alarmed or desperate or boring strangers back to the house from her random samplings of different places and acts of worship.

Gran had forced Francis and Pat to get out much more.

They could not endure her pity at the start of their rare coincidental weekends off, when they were prepared to settle in to two days of doing nothing much, and she ran them through her commitments. She was a freelance indexer of

historical works, and a self-ap-
pointed tidier of graves and
churches, so the kitchen and living
room were convenient spaces for
setting out the details of a reign, a
battle, a marriage or a plot.

The rubbish bin and waste-paper
baskets overflowed with the things
Francis's grandmother had found
unfitting in church or cemetery,
gloves or cans or inspirational paper-
backs, silver-paper horseshoes and
ballpoint pens.

'Don't put down that pot!' Gran
shrieked to Pat, as he tried to fetch
Francis's tea in the morning. 'You
could unsettle the Anabaptists!'

While they were out at work, Pat
at the restaurant and Francis driving

the laundry around, Gran covered
any space there was with $3 \times 5''$
index cards and blue post-its. Both
Francis and Pat worked shifts, so
they never knew if the other had
even attempted to release some
space from the formation of battle
at Oudenarde, the machinations of
the Cabal or Ironbridge Telford's
gazetted surviving works. When
they got in they either fetched
something to eat and took it up to
bed, or rushed out, feeling illicit and
safe. Very rarely, they shared a
precarious feast with Francis's
grandmother.

In a way, Gran had brought back
the cramped romantic first days of
their love, when they had nothing

to hide because no one would have believed even if they'd written it out loud all over the bathroom mirror. They were such good friends, friends from their perambulators, more like brothers. This was the line still adopted by Francis's mother, Kay, who hoovered between the feet of her husband as he sat in his chair, and always baked double to freeze half in case of sudden guests.

It was fortunate that Francis had always loved Pat, since there'd been no sudden guest, ever, within a cherry's spit of their house.

Sometimes at night Pat would make a meal for Francis and Gran, picking his way between the bits of information on paper and the birds' nests of ecclesiastical leavings. He would recreate what he had served in the restaurant earlier. Although he wasn't yet a chef, he had the curiosity and steady hands for it; he worked so hard it was really only a matter of time before he got the promotion. He was at the stage now when you did the one thing over and over till you could do it in your sleep – if you got any, that was. It seemed oddly miniature to him to concoct meals just for Francis and his grandmother, an eccentric hobby nothing much to do with work. Himself, he ate through the pores all day and could barely stand food at the end of it. He ate smoke and drank water. When he saw Francis's thickening waist, he was proud of it.

'I made that,' he'd say to Gran, who would reply, 'Much to be proud of there,' and join Pat outside the lean-to for a cig after whatever rich meal the boy had made.

All very comfortable, until just recently, when Kay had started on about the calls she was getting from dissatisfied authors.

'They say Mother's having them on. Either that, or she's losing her accuracy,' she said to Pat, whom she'd rung at the restaurant, sure of getting a better hearing than she would from her own son. 'You can't do work for other people and be inaccurate. They plain don't like it. It shows them up.'

'Perhaps she means to,' said Pat, which was no more than what he thought.

'She's always been scrupulous about her research. She even stores her thoughts alphabetically. If you ask about the car you don't have to wait as long as if you ask her about Francis. And if I ask about you there's a slightly longer wait while she locates P.'

'She's maybe tired of sorting other people's words.'

'If you like it, it's not the sort of thing you go off,' said Kay. 'I should know, I've never cared a fig for it and still don't.'

Since she was not Pat's mother, he was not as irked by her angle as Francis would have been.

He approached Francis.

'Do you think your grandmother's losing it?' he asked.

'Nope. She may have a project on, though.' Francis had walked back from the depot where he had left the van. He was determined to do something about it before he had to change his waist size for good. He'd give Pat a surprise.

'Try one of these. Red pepper straws. A bit of Gruyère and several dozen eggs.' Pat had made them specially, but pretended he'd brought them from work. Gran was upstairs working on an overcrowded letter 'V' in a work on the history of lenses and their effect on art history, whose author was at that moment enjoying some of Pat's cheese straws brought home by his wife in her handbag, after a business lunch.

'What type of project?' asked Pat.

'I think she's trying to get sent to a home.'

'No one does that. It's lonely, and it costs all you've got, no matter how much you've got. The body only gives out when it's cried all it can and spent all there is.'

'*You* say that,' said Francis, kissing him. 'But I think she's being tactful. That's why my mother's so tactless she could perform amputations with her afterthoughts. Because *her* mother's so tactful she makes everyone believe she's the one at fault, not them.'

'But no one wants to go into a home. Have you seen inside one? Home is what they're not. They can't call them what they are. Asylum is a lovely word in every way compared with what they are.'

'Maybe she's got some idea of going to a place where she can think it all out and then just lie down and float off. *I* don't know.'

'Bed's that place,' said Pat, who hated being alone and could not sort through his memories for very long without meeting Francis there,

and fearing the day when they
would not be within reach of one
another.

'And move! And bend! And stretch!'
sang the voice at the centre of the
house, unsexed as a parrot. Mary
walked up the right flank of the
outside staircase up to the façade
and looked in through the ballroom window.

Accompanied by a piano, the old
men and women in nightwear or
loose combinations of cotton followed the gestures of the strong fit
body, wielding a smart black cane,
that called to them. In their move-
ments they gave hints of what they
saw, like quiet flightless birds. They

did not dance or exercise so much as talk with their hands, their necks, their knees, remembering longer, more abandoned, gestures they had once made.

The room smelled of powder and pads, and the unkind reek of setting lotion. The hairdresser had been that morning to see to the hair of the women. His visit was less to do with appearance than appearances. The old men hid in the smoking room when the hairdresser came, in order to set up their own evil pong.

It was while the perms and sets and demiwaves were taking shape on a Thursday that Mary was able to join Mr Charteris in the pantry.

He had won her with his golden tongue.

'You're new,' he said. 'I always show the new maids the ropes.'

She knew better than to correct his words. A number of them, being old, spoke like old people couldn't help but do. She'd a lot of time for old people. She'd worked in several homes before, though none as exclusive – meaning expensive – as this. Some of them paid their own bills, others got paid for by children, not without a grumble at the end of the month.

Mr Charteris had arrangements, and that was all Mary had heard, though she had heard one old trout call him a 'scholarship boy' and then whinny with the pleasure being unpleasant gives to those who do not fight it.

Mr Charteris continued: 'Any difficulties at all with the other girls, come straight to me. Don't waste your time going to Mrs How's Yer Father or troubling old Oojamaflip.' He twisted the stud under his bow tie and then level-led off its ends. 'There's nothing I can't tell you about the house. Nothing at all. Man and boy I've been here, starting in the carpenter's yard on crackbacked chairs and coming right through till I got where I am now.'

Mary was unsure what a person might want to know about a house, and where exactly Mr Charteris had got to.

'God, it must be old if *you've* been here all along,' she said, and was delighted when he laughed. He had assertive teeth, every one his own.

'I followed on after only five others like myself. That's not many butlers over the two-seventy-odd years. Not that the earlier ones could rightly be called butlers.'

Mary, who understood from the television that butlers were men who stood still, sneered, and talked posh, asked, 'The work can't have been hard, though?'

Mr Charteris considered the mornings of his life when he, at much the age of this girl, had collaborated in the daily launch of the house, cleaned, polished, dazzling, rebegun, all on the sweat of eight men and sixteen girls, repeating with their bodies actions of the most tedious and exhausting kind in order to give a context to the ease of others, like men blowing bottles from the burning roots of their lungs just to hold scent that would waft off an earlobe unnoticed in the breeze.

'I've had a woman in every room of the house,' said Mr Charteris to Mary.

He revisited the house in the way he preferred in his mind, through the oxters and ribbons and stays and mouthings of the Roses, Daisys, Rubys, Violets, Marias and Elizas who had been drawn by him into each room's mystery, so that he understood the attic through Hetty's red hair and startling milky snores, the music room through the stifled tears and later laughter of Lavender as he lowered the music stool slowly beneath her by swivelling the mahogany discs at either side within her skirts, the ballroom by the chilly biting of Daphne as they pushed together inside the curtains, the kitchen through the blissful humming of Euphemia's skin under his mouth, and later through the regrettable harrying of his own late wife.

'Every room?' said Mary, not interested, nor paying attention, really, not having listened, as people often do not to the old. She just couldn't help, being a trained geriatric nurse, running with the feeble thread. When she found it attached to a cunning rope she was caught by her own decency, the first snare.

Knowing well the sunshine it is to be needed, even by someone who means little, and sensing his distinct, perhaps unrepeatable, advantage, Mr Charteris said to Mary, relying on her tenderness and on his own undimmed brown eyes, 'Every room, my dear, except the pantry.'

These afternoons, the little treats of food given privately, the counterfeit tasks undertaken by Mr Charteris in the aftermath of his making good

that late omission, went on beyond
the one time it would in principle
have taken. Who could say whether
Mary had not learned from the old
man, just before he sank, the radiant
satisfaction of domestic habit, that it
was not she who escaped from
regulation and certainty into the
life of the back of the house, into
invented duties and words that were
as plain and mysterious as the low
windows giving out on to the deeps
of the park where no one went any
more, or not so that it was known?

The back stairs of the house were
cool even in this heat. The service lift
creaked on its cables down past the
stone stairs to Francis, where he stood

with the laundry hamper poised on its mobile ramp, ready to load. He pushed the creaking thing in to the lift, and pulled on the cables, calling upwards, 'All yours, Mary.'

He heard her tug and brake on the cables, and ran up the stone stairs to her, ready to pull out the hamper and help her roll it to the laundry room on the pallet on casters that stood ready in the top corridor. The floors were timber, not lino, up here.

'Come and help me sort it if you can spare the time,' said Mary. 'It's beautiful work.'

He supposed at first that she spoke that way on account of having a vocation, as he supposed a nurse must.

But the work *was* beautiful today in the laundry room, its high brief windows letting light in from both sides of the roof, the shelves and wooden floor smelling of dry lavender and lavender wax. Mary and Francis pulled out sleeve after heavy sleeve of laundered white sheet.

'We could do the laundry here if it was brought up to date. There's the room, but no machines. They'd cost. But Lord knows what you cost.'

'It's not rightly me. I drive the van. They wash the sheets.'

'You know what I mean.'

'You look well today, Mary,' said Francis, certain he would not be misunderstood. 'You always look well. It must be encouraging for the residents.'

'Thanks,' said Mary. 'All I am is alive.'

Outside two pigeons skirmished in a lead gutter, the green and pink off their breasts firing through the old glass, their exalted cooing boastful.

'I've a grandmother living at home with me and my friend at the moment. She works with papers. Lately there have been complaints that she's losing her grip. I don't think she is. I think she's being tactful.'

'Tactful?' Mary pushed a pile of sheets to the back of a shelf. It moved with a toppling weight over the papered shelf and then settled against the white wall. 'Who to?'

'In case my friend and I want a bit of space.'

'Do you now?'

'Well, we wouldn't mind *space*. She covers everything with bits of paper. And she brings home worshippers of whatever denomination has irritated her recently.'

'Irritated her?'

'By keeping a messy churchyard. Or, if she can get in, an untidy church. They tend to be rural. She reaches those by bus.'

'She brings them home?'

'Yes, you know. After she's tidied up the place of worship, she attends a service or two and then lures them

38

home. They sit and talk. She draws them out. They frequently return. We've made a number of friends.'

'So she is active and sociable?'

Francis did not like the sound of those words. They described human traits with a functional tongue.

'I love her. When I say we could do with a bit more space, that's all I mean. She takes up a certain amount of room. I want her with us, unless she wants to be away herself. How do I find out what she wants? I don't believe her work *is* slipping. I don't see it. I've only my mother's word for it. Chuck me those draw sheets and I'll go up the steps.'

'You want to know what she wants?'

'I want to know what she wants.'

'Bring her here to look. It's one of the best. The place is beautiful. She could fill her whole room – they get a room to themselves, you know – with pieces of paper. She could have visitors. At least between certain hours. Not in the evening. They get a bath when they want, as long as it's twice a week and they don't use bath oil. That ups the fractures and *that* looks bad. They don't have shepherd's pie every single day. Sister doesn't always open their letters. The toilets have emergency bells that get an annual service. There's a weekly hairdresser. There are socials.'

'It sounds great,' said Francis, his heart flat.

'Yes,' said Mary, 'and it's not free either.'

Francis's grandmother replaced the telephone. She enjoyed the fact that her daughter Kay did not recognise her when she called up in the voice of a learned and exasperated historian or an angry man of letters who had made allowances for an old woman long enough.

Indexing had at last lost its charm for Lavender Maclehose. She had it in mind to get away, and to use the part of her savings she had not earmarked for these two dear good boys. There was the funeral account tidied up, with the undertaker at last convinced about her plan of having confetti and mimosa – whatever the time of year – and making sure that six dozen pink roses were left behind in the vestry for the cleaner.

'I'm home,' called her grandson. 'Do you fancy a cig while I cut a lettuce?'

'Delicious,' said his grandmother, hoping it would do for whatever he had said. So much of her time now was spent day-dreaming. She had it planned. It would be soon. Her knowledge of rural buses would help.

It was still light in the small garden. Francis cut a pale crinkled lettuce. It left a woody boss, weeping milk. He lit his grandmother's cigarette and looked at the gardens

beyond, the wigwams of runner
beans with their red flowers, the
tipsy roses and tired children refus-
ing to leave their darkening climb-
ing frames.

'Don't ever think you must leave
unless it's what you want,' he said to
his grandmother. 'We've all the
room in the world here for you,
you know that. Pretend I haven't
said this.'

Pat had brought the perfect dinner
for the three of them off the last
shift. They sat in the silvery narrow
garden. There was cold soup made
out of herbs and cream, a cheese the
size of a flat iron, and two slices of
a kind of berry cake. They burned a

khaki candle to keep off the gnats. It was an old citronella candle from the ironmongery where Francis had once worked. They had enough nails for life.

Lavender had taken care not to tidy up in any depth before she ran away. She said goodnight to Pat and to Francis in her usual brusque fashion, even remembering to cross the bedroom floor again and again as she did most nights.

When she was sure they were asleep, she took her grip and left the two letters on the kitchen counter, beside the kettle. One for her daughter, one for the two men.

She closed the door with a dog-owner's stealth.

The street was drenched with dew and lamplight as she walked down it and out towards the bypass.

It was too early for milkfloats, too late for country buses. She walked more quickly than she had for years. With no one to watch her, she was again young as she made her way to the road that led to the house she had known before Kay was born, the house where she had worked so hard she vowed to work with her brain only, ever after, so that she had worked nights to become a house-keeper of books, a spring-cleaner of the alphabet.

She was on her way back to the house that she had come to miss as you miss the use of your young body, the house she was ready to reinhabit at the end. She dreamed as she made her way along the awakening road of working again at the dusting and ceaseless polishing of wood, the testing of the fine furniture to see it was all in working order so that others might use it, others who did not know that on the piano stool where sat little Miss Veronica there had only that morning been a spin and a flurry at the heart of a whirl of petticoats scented with nothing more rare than lavender wax.

A NOTE ON THE AUTHOR

Candia McWilliam is the author of
three novels, the most recent of which,
Debatable Land, won the *Guardian*
Fiction Prize. She lives in Oxford.

ALSO AVAILABLE AS BLOOMSBURY QUIDS

Margaret Atwood	*The Labrador Fiasco*
T. Coraghessan Boyle	*She Wasn't Soft*
Nadine Gordimer	*Harald, Claudia, and their Son Duncan*
David Guterson	*The Drowned Son*
Jay McInerney	*The Queen and I*
Will Self	*A Story for Europe*
Patrick Süskind	*Maître Mussard's Bequest*
Joanna Trollope	*Faith*
Tobias Wolff	*Two Boys and a Girl*

AVAILABLE AS BLOOMSBURY CLASSICS

Jimmy and the Desperate Woman, D. H. Lawrence
Einstein's Dreams, Alan Lightman
Bright Lights, Big City, Jay McInerney
Debatable Land, Candia McWilliam
Bliss and Other Stories, Katherine Mansfield
The Garden Party and Other Stories, Katherine Mansfield
So Far from God, Patrick Marnham
Lies of Silence, Brian Moore
The Lonely Passion of Judith Hearne, Brian Moore
The Pumpkin Eater, Penelope Mortimer
Lives of Girls and Women, Alice Munro
The Country Girls, Edna O'Brien
Coming Through Slaughter, Michael Ondaatje
The English Patient, Michael Ondaatje
In the Skin of a Lion, Michael Ondaatje
Running in the Family, Michael Ondaatje
Let Them Call it Jazz, Jean Rhys
Wide Sargasso Sea, Jean Rhys
Keepers of the House, Lisa St Aubin de Téran
The Quantity Theory of Insanity, Will Self
The Pigeon, Patrick Süskind
The Heather Blazing, Colm Tóibín
Cocktails at Doney's and Other Stories, William Trevor
The Choir, Joanna Trollope
Angel, All Innocence, Fay Weldon
Oranges are not the only fruit, Jeanette Winterson
The Passion, Jeanette Winterson
Sexing the Cherry, Jeanette Winterson
In Pharaoh's Army, Tobias Wolff
This Boy's Life, Tobias Wolff
Orlando, Virginia Woolf
A Room of One's Own, Virginia Woolf